W9-BRC-464

# Let's Go Apple Picking!

By Molly Kempf

Illustrated by SI Artists, Josie Yee, Jim Durk, and Lisa Workman

Grosset & Dunlap

ISBN 978-0-448-44668-4          10 9 8 7 6 5 4 3 2 1

Strawberry Shortcake was berry excited! It was a crisp fall day in Strawberryland and she was taking Apple Dumplin' apple picking after breakfast.

Strawberry knew that her friends would be out picking apples, too. Everyone was planning to make special apple treats for the next day's Autumn Harvest Festival.

Strawberry put Apple Dumplin' into her wagon and headed for Apple Blossom Orchard.

"I know exactly what to make for the Harvest Festival, Apple!" Strawberry said with a smile. "A spiced apple cake with cream-cheese frosting!"

"Cake!" said Apple Dumplin' as she clapped her hands happily. Apple cake was one of her favorite treats!

By the time Strawberry and Apple Dumplin' arrived at the orchard, Angel Cake had already picked a basket full of apples.

"Hi, Angel!" Strawberry called.

"Can't talk now, Strawberry," Angel Cake said quickly. "I've got to get home to make spiced apple cake for tomorrow. Bye!"

Berry Trail

"Angel makes the berry best apple cake! I can't make the same thing," Strawberry said as Angel walked away. "I know! I'm sure everyone will be thirsty. I can make fresh apple juice!"

Just as Strawberry lifted up her sister to
pick an apple, Orange Blossom arrived.

"Hi, Orange! Are you ready for the Harvest
Festival?" Strawberry asked.

"Yup!" Orange answered excitedly. "I'm
making cinnamon apple juice."

"I was going to make apple juice, too," Strawberry said. "But now I think I'll make caramel apples instead!"

"Yum!" Orange said as she picked a few ripe apples and then headed off to a different part of the orchard.

Just then Ginger Snap, Huckleberry Pie, and Blueberry Muffin came over to say hello.

"Wow!" said Ginger, picking a juicy red apple. "These will be perfect for my caramel apples! I'd better get going."

I can't make caramel apples if Ginger
is making them, Strawberry thought.
Hmm, maybe I'll make an apple pie. After
all, everyone loves apple pie!

"These apples will be great in my apple pie, too!" said Huck, taking a bite of a crunchy apple. "See you later."

"I can't wait to try your apple pie, Huck," said Blueberry.

Then both girls waved good-bye to Huck as he left the orchard.

"I was going to make an apple pie," Strawberry said, trying not to sound too upset.

"You'll think of something else!" Blueberry said brightly. She giggled and added, "Just not apple muffins—I'm making those."

"That sounds berry yummy!" Strawberry
said, giggling too. "You're right—I'm sure I'll
think of the perfect treat."

Strawberry and Apple Dumplin' gathered one last basket of apples. But Strawberry couldn't stop worrying about what to make for the festival.

*What if I'm the only one who doesn't have a treat to bring?* thought Strawberry sadly. *I just have to come up with something!*

When Strawberry and Apple got home, they carried all of their apples into the kitchen. "Apples!" cooed Apple Dumplin' excitedly.

"That's right, sweetie. Apples for Apple Dumplin',"
said Strawberry, hugging her sister.

Suddenly, Strawberry had a berry wonderful idea. "I
know just what to make. Let's get cooking!"

Strawberry and Apple Dumplin' worked all afternoon. They peeled and sliced and seasoned, and soon the kitchen was filled with delicious smells.

The next morning, the girls packed up their surprise and went to the Autumn Harvest Festival. All of their friends were there playing games and sharing delicious apple treats.

"This is the best Harvest Festival ever!" exclaimed Strawberry happily.

"So what did you end up making with all of your apples, Strawberry?" asked Blueberry.

"I made Apple Dumplin's berry favorite treat—apple dumplings!" exclaimed Strawberry. Strawberry smiled to herself. She couldn't imagine a better way to celebrate the autumn harvest than with her berry best friends!